The UNITED NATIONS

Nicolas Brasch

Australia • Brazil • Japan • Korea • Mexico • Singapore • Spain • United Kingdom • United States

The United Nations

Fast Forward
Green Level 14

Text: Nicolas Brasch
Editor: Johanna Rohan
Design: Stella Vassiliou
Series design: James Lowe
Production controller: Emma Hayes
Photo research: Corrina Tauschke
Audio recordings: Juliet Hill, Picture Start
Spoken by: Matthew King and Abbe Holmes

Acknowledgements
The author and publisher would like to acknowledge permission to reproduce material from the following sources: Photographs by AAP Image/Justin Lane, p 7 inset; Getty Images Editorial/Don Emmert/AFP, p 19/ George Rodger Time Life Pictures, p 10/Gianluigi Guerica/AFP, p 15 top/Herbert Orth/Time Life Pictures, p 6/ Hulton Archive Stringer, back cover, p 12/ Margaret Bourke-White/Time Life Pictures, p 11/ Nat Farbman/Time Life Pictures, p 6 inset/ Picture Post/Hulton Archive, p 13/ Sophia Paris/UN/Minustah, p 14 bottom; Photo Edit/Rudi Von Briel, p 5; Photolibrary.com/Henryk T Kaiser, p 4/ Mick Roessier, p 22/ Picture Finders, cover, pp 1, 3, 23; UN Photo, pp 18-19/ Ky Chung, p 14 top/ Eskinder Debebe, p 16/ Sophia Paris, pp 7, 17/ B Wolff, p 15 bottom.

ISBN 978 0 17 012592 5
ISBN 978 0 17 012585 7 (set)

Cengage Learning Australia
Level 7, 80 Dorcas Street
South Melbourne, Victoria Australia 3205
Phone: 1300 790 853

Cengage Learning New Zealand
Unit 4B Rosedale Office Park
331 Rosedale Road, Albany, North Shore NZ 0632
Phone: 0800 449 725

For learning solutions, visit **cengage.com.au**

Printed in Australia by Ligare Pty Ltd
10 11 12 13 14 15 16 19 18 17 16 15

THE UNIVERSITY OF
MELBOURNE

Evaluated in independent research by staff from the Department of Language, Literacy and Arts Education at the University of Melbourne.

The UNITED NATIONS

Nicolas Brasch

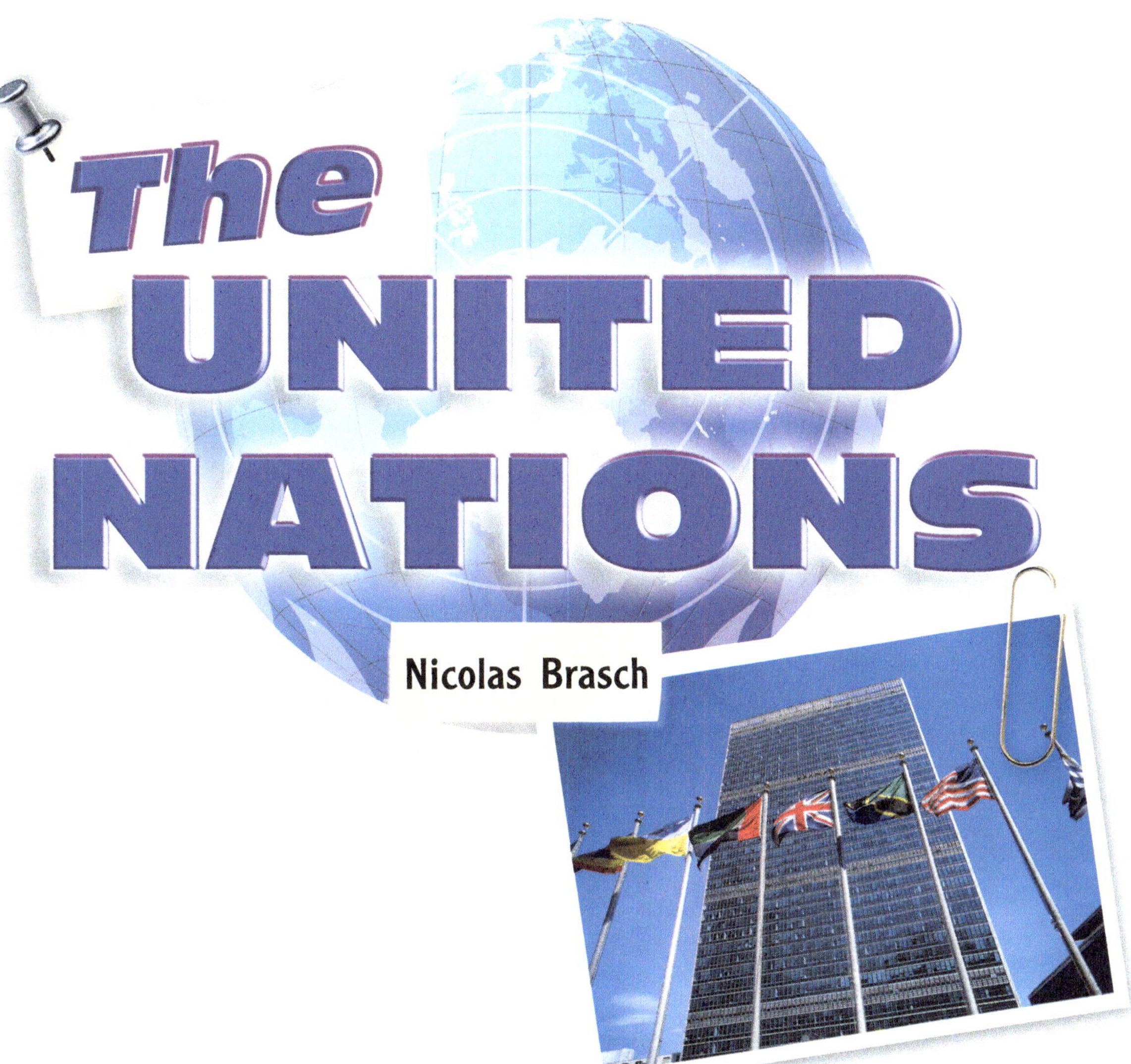

Contents

Chapter 1	**The United Nations**	4
Chapter 2	**Members**	6
Chapter 3	**Forming the United Nations**	10
Chapter 4	**What the United Nations Does**	14
Chapter 5	**Making Decisions**	18
Chapter 6	**Visiting**	22
Glossary and Index		24

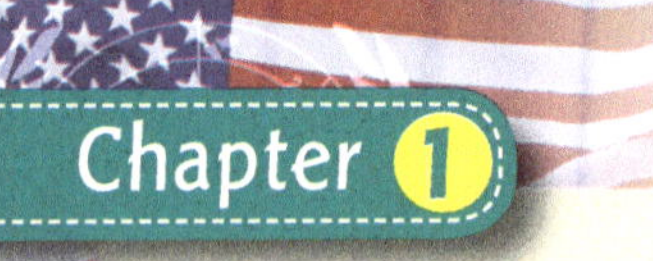

Chapter 1

THE UNITED NATIONS

The United Nations is an **organisation** that tries to solve problems around the world.

It helps poor countries and rich countries. It helps big countries and small countries.

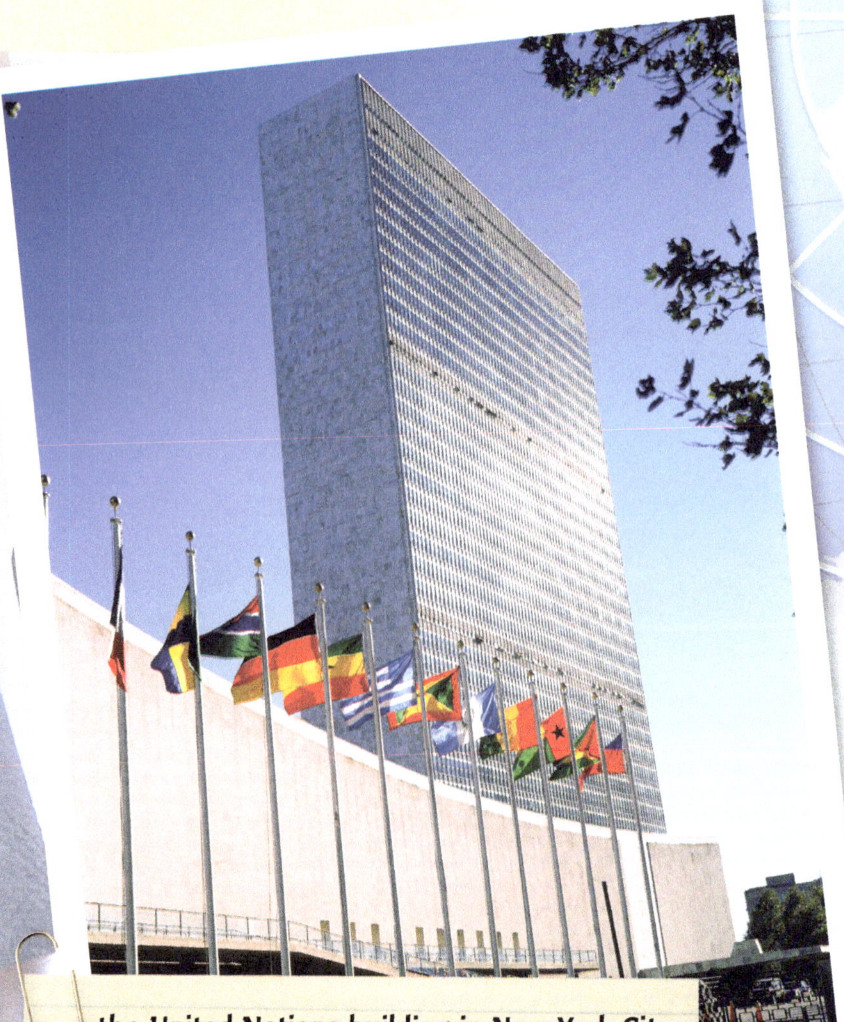

the United Nations building in New York City

The United Nations tries to make the world a fairer, and more peaceful place to live.

All of the aims of the United Nations can be found in the United Nations **Charter**.

The United Nations logo is a map of the world with olive branches around it.

Olive branches are a sign of peace.

MEMBERS

The United Nations Charter says that all peace-loving states or countries can become members as long as they respect the decisions of the United Nations.

CHARTER OF THE UNITED NATIONS

WE THE PEOPLES OF THE UNITED NATIONS
DETERMINED

to save succeeding generations from the scourge of war, which twice in our lifetime has brought untold sorrow to mankind, and

to reaffirm faith in fundamental human rights, in the dignity and worth of the human person, in the equal rights of men and women and of nations large and small, and

to establish conditions under which justice and respect for the obligations arising from treaties and other sources of international law can be maintained, and

to promote social progress and better standards of life in larger freedom,

AND FOR THESE ENDS

to practice tolerance and live together in peace with one another as good neighbors, and

to unite our strength to maintain international peace and security, and

to ensure, by the acceptance of principles and the institution of methods, that armed force shall not be used, save in the common interest, and

to employ international machinery for the promotion of the economic and social advancement of all peoples,

HAVE RESOLVED TO COMBINE OUR EFFORTS
TO ACCOMPLISH THESE AIMS.

Accordingly, our respective Governments, through representativ the city of San Francisco, who have exhibited their full powers fou and due form, have agreed to the present Charter of the Unite hereby establish an international organization to be known as th

It's the aim of all members to keep peace in the world.

United Nations
Secretary-General Kofi Annan

Today, 191 countries belong to the United Nations. That's most of the countries in the world.

these countries are some of the members of the United Nations

Any country can become a member
of the United Nations,
as long as they follow the rules
in the Charter.

Running Words 155

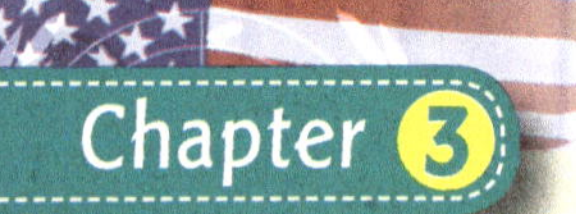

FORMING THE UNITED NATIONS

The United Nations was formed after **World War II**.

The events of World War II were terrible for many countries.
No one wanted to have another war like it.

In June 1945, representatives from 50 countries met in the USA to form an organisation that would help to stop another big war.

The United Nations was formed on 24 October 1945. United Nations Day is held each year on 24 October.

Chapter 4

WHAT THE UNITED NATIONS DOES

The United Nations does a lot of different things for people around the world.

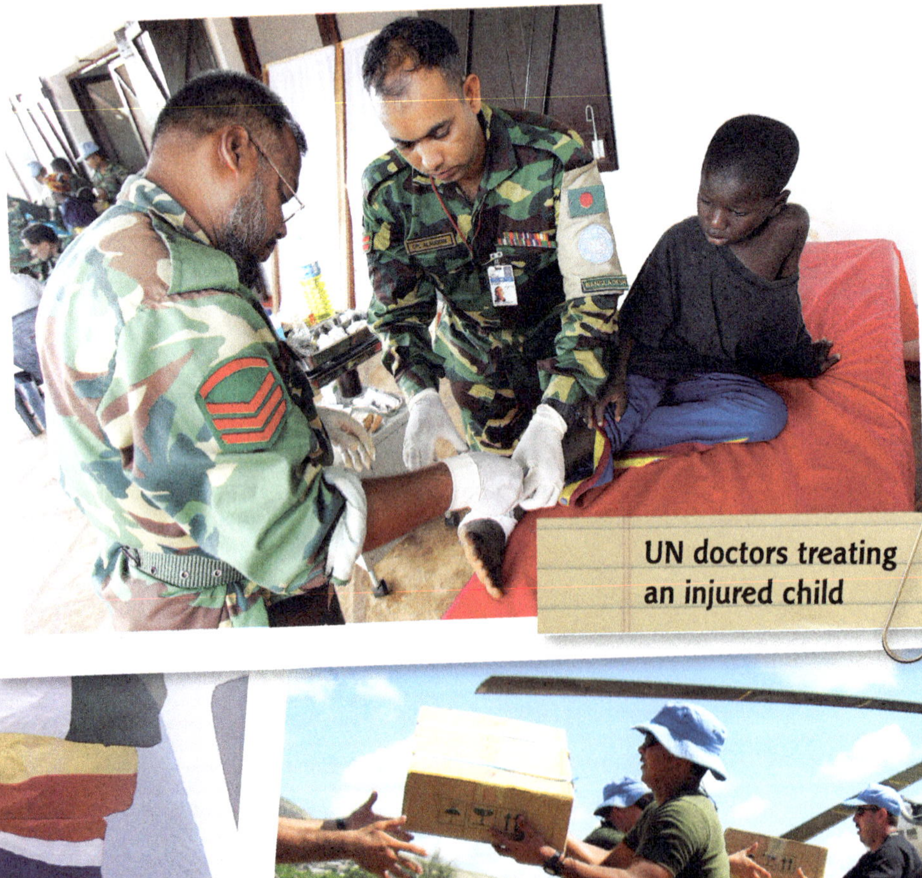

UN doctors treating an injured child

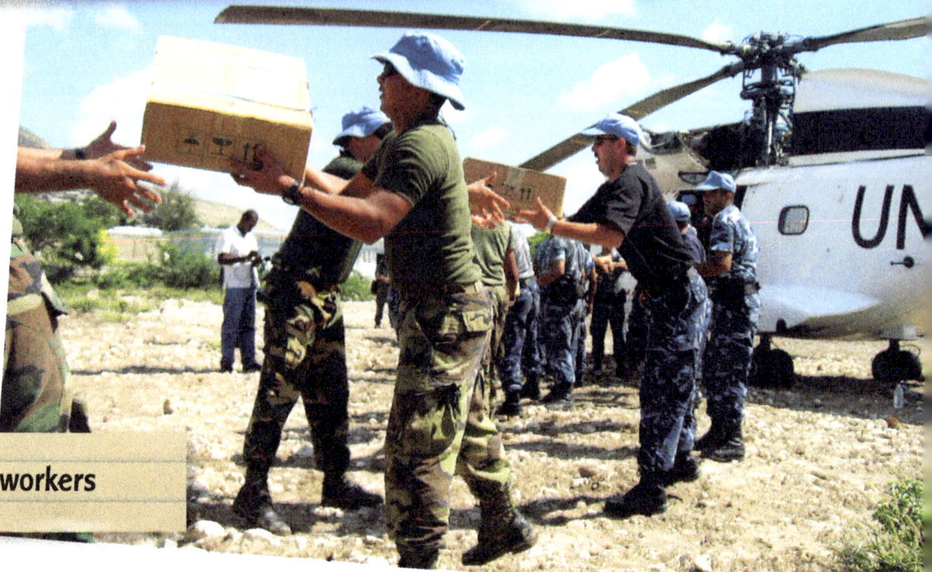

UN aid workers

a UN peacekeeper handing out food

The United Nations helps to feed people who have little food.

It helps to educate people in places where there are no schools.

children at school

The United Nations keeps a close watch on governments that don't treat all of their people in the same way.

The United Nations sends **peacekeepers** to countries where there has been fighting.

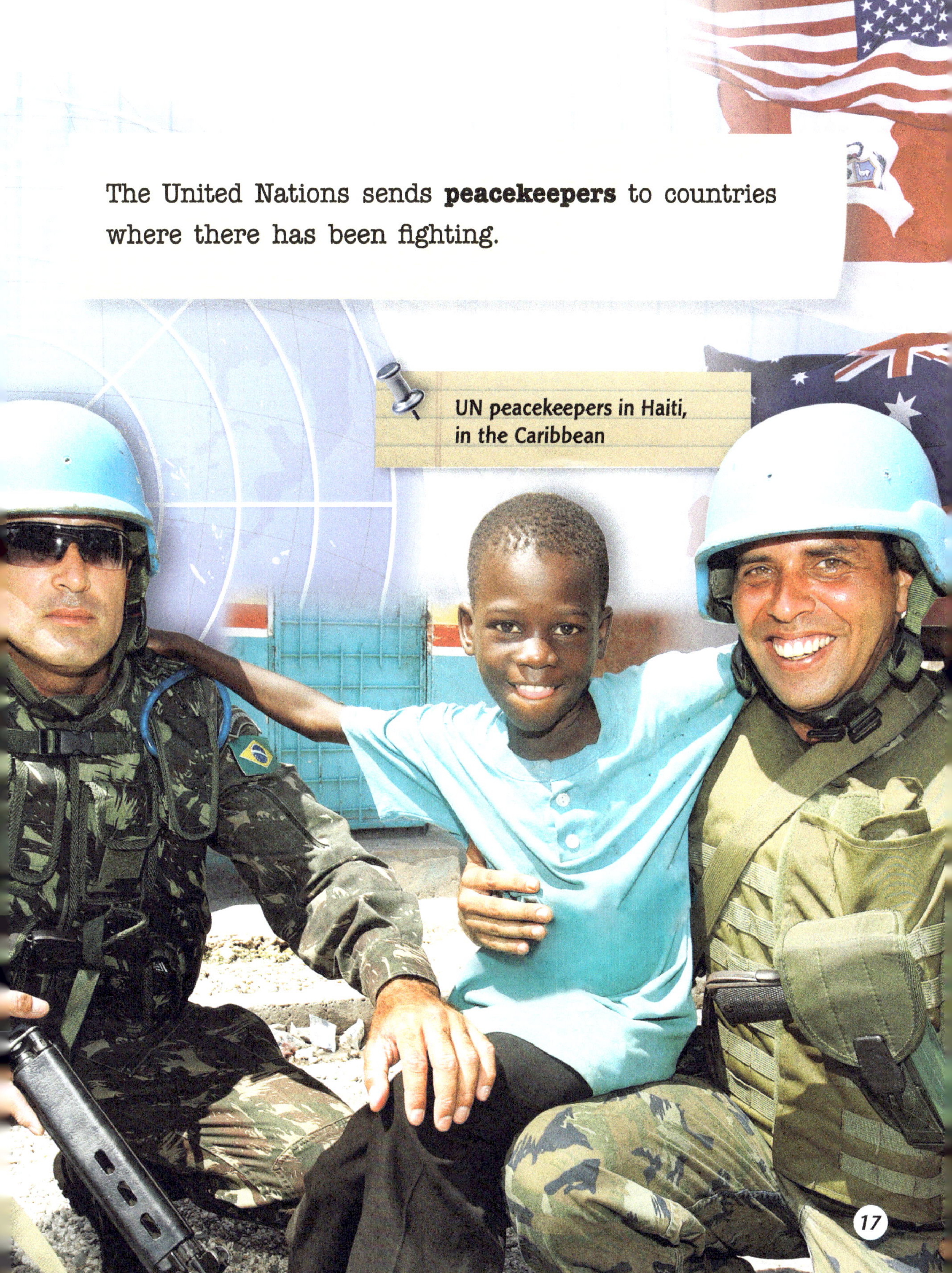

UN peacekeepers in Haiti, in the Caribbean

MAKING DECISIONS

The **General Assembly** of the United Nations makes most of the important decisions for the organisation.

The General Assembly is made up of representatives from the 191 members of the United Nations.

Each member of the United Nations has one vote on every matter that is talked about.

There are five countries in the United Nations that each have the power to stop a decision being made.

This is called the **veto** power.

The countries with the veto power are:

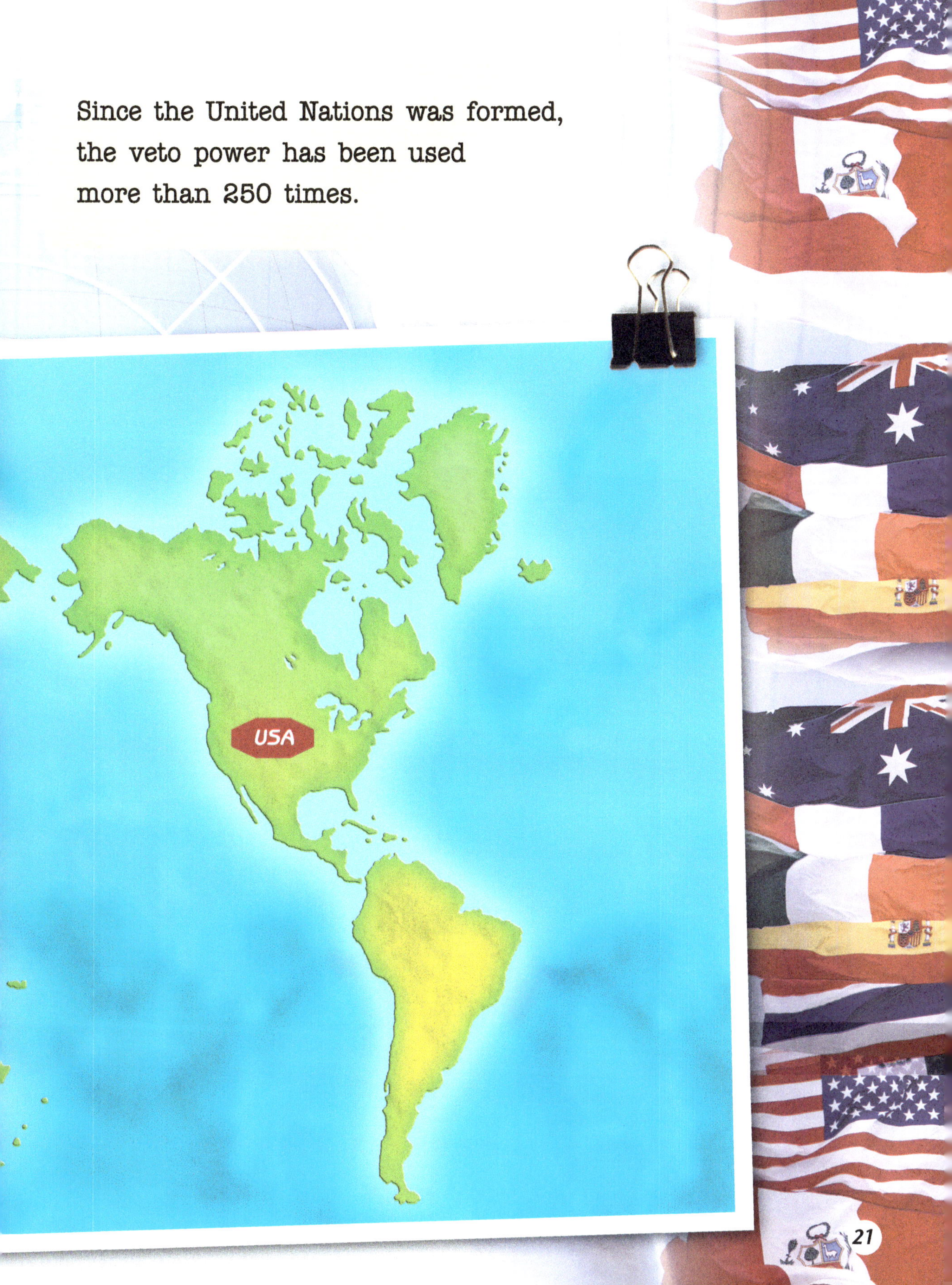

Since the United Nations was formed, the veto power has been used more than 250 times.

Chapter 6

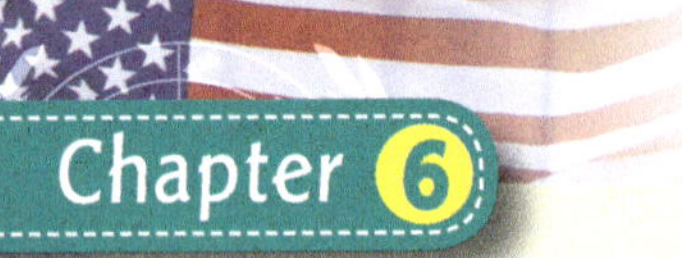

VISITING

The head office of the United Nations is in New York City, in the USA. The head office is where the General Assembly meets and votes.

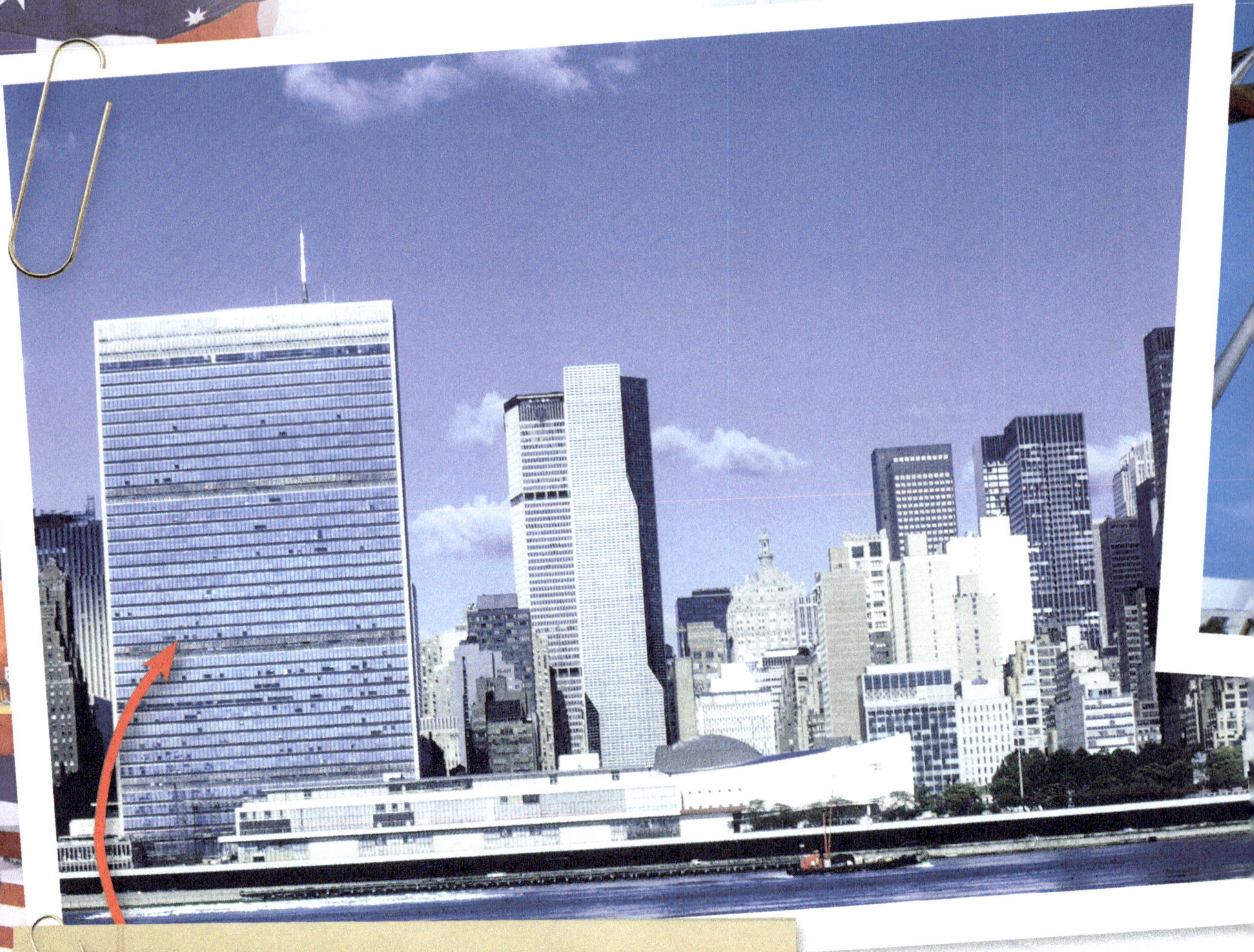

the United Nations' head office in New York City

Outside the United Nations' head office are the flags of every member's country.
The first flag is Afghanistan
and the last flag is Zimbabwe.

Glossary

charter	a written description of an organisation's functions
General Assembly	the main body of the United Nations. It serves as a forum for members to discuss important issues.
organisation	an organised body of people
peacekeepers	people who are sent to an area to help keep the peace
veto	the right to reject a decision
World War II	a war involving many countries fought between 1939 – 1945

Index

Afganistan 23

General Assembly 18, 22

Haiti 17

New York City 4, 22

United Nations Charter 5, 6, 9

World War II 10–11

Zimbabwe 23